SKATEBOARD STUNT
DANGER ZONE

FANTAIL PUBLISHING,
AN IMPRINT OF PUFFIN ENTERPRISES

Published by the Penguin Group
27 Wrights Lane, London W8 5TZ England

Viking Penguin Inc., 375 Hudson Street, New York, New York
10014, USA.
Penguin Books Australia Ltd. Ringwood, Victoria, Australia.
Penguin Books Canada Ltd., 2801 John Street, Markham,
Ontario, Canada LR3 1BA.
Penguin Books (NZ) Ltd., 182-190 Wairau Road Auckland 10
New Zealand.
Penguin Books Ltd., Registered Offices: Harmondsworth,
Middlesex, England.

First Published by The Berkley Publishing Group 1990
First Published in the UK by Penguin Books 1990

10 9 8 7 6 5 4 3 2 1

Copyright © 1990 by Palladium Media Enterprises, Inc.

SKATEBOARD STUNT

A Novel by Nancy E. Krulik
Based on the Al Burton Production LASSIE
Adapted from the episode "THE
SKATEBOARD SAGA "
Written by Dave Meyer

CHAPTER
1

WHOOSH! The skateboard soared off the steep homemade ramp at high speed. As the board hit the ground below, its rider bent his knees, raised his arms, and tilted his body slightly to the left to take the turn without falling. He stood slowly as he reached the end of the course, and the skateboard skidded to a stop.

"Yeah! All right!" The crowd of boys that had gathered to watch their friend ride his board on the ramp ran over to cheer him on.

"Nice going!"

"Awesome!"

"Hacksaw, you are the coolest!"

Hacksaw didn't even smile back at his adoring fans, never mind offer them a word of thanks. Hacksaw was a tough kid. He was twelve years old, about two years older than most of the other boys who had gathered at the homemade ramp. Hacksaw was an expert skateboarder, but he took too many chances. He always rode his board without wearing a helmet or protective pads, and he always set up dangerous homemade skateboard courses in unsafe places. It had been Hacksaw's idea to build the rickety, wobbly, quarter-pipe ramp he had just taken off from in the first place.

The boys had all worked together to build the ramp. Well, almost all of them. Hacksaw himself didn't do any of the physical labor. He stood off to the side barking orders to the others.

The ramp led right into a road that was closed off to traffic while it was being repaired. The road backed into an old reservoir which had been drained for the time being, so the workmen could complete their work on the road.

When Hacksaw was through showing off on the ramp, he decided to demonstrate his talents by skating along the base of the reservoir that stood at the end of the road. The reservoir was blocked off by a chainlink fence, but Hacksaw found a part of the fence that had been knocked down by the wind and could be climbed over easily. Some of the younger boys hadn't wanted to climb over the rickety old aluminum chainlink fence. But Hacksaw had dared them to climb it, and because none of the boys wanted to be called a chicken, they had all followed the older boy over the fence and into the reservoir.

So within a few minutes, most of the boys were happily skateboarding around the base of the reservoir at top speed, shrieking with delight. Some of the more experienced skateboarders were taking off from the upper lip of the reservoir and attempting daring midair poses before landing in the base of the reservoir.

Ten-year-old Will McCulloch and his faithful brown and white purebred collie, Lassie, stood on the other side of the chainlink fence, watching the kids as they rode. Will stared enviously at the group of laughing, shouting skateboarders.

"Lucky guys," he said with more than just a touch of jealousy in his voice. Will loved riding skateboards. Unfortunately, right now his board was broken.

Lassie rubbed up against her master's leg and whined. Will looked down at Lassie and petted the soft white spot at the top of her head. "Forget it, Lassie," he said with a laugh. "You're not getting on any skateboard."

Will pulled his bike up closer to the fence to get a better look at the quarter-pipe ramp. Lassie followed close at his heels. As Will stuck his face up against the metal fence, he was met by Hacksaw's icy stare.

"Better not get too close," Hacksaw said, laughing mockingly. "You might get hurt."

It was all Will could do to manage a small, shaky smile back at Hacksaw. Will wasn't afraid of getting hurt by a runaway skateboard. He was more afraid of getting hurt by this older bully who was staring him down.

Hacksaw laughed again and then took off to skate around the base. Will watched the kids ride for a while. He was so engrossed in their moves that he didn't even notice when Lassie left his side and trotted a few yards up the side of the hill.

"Ruff! Ruff!" Lassie called to Will.

Will turned toward his dog. "What is it, girl?" Will called up to her as he walked his bike over to Lassie to get a good look at what had upset her so.

"Ruff! Ruff!" Lassie barked again, using her head to point to a small, ground-level concrete flood channel that held the water back from the reservoir.

Will looked from the channel to the skateboarders. "I know it's dangerous," he admitted to Lassie. "But sometimes you have to look the other way. Besides, I'm sure someone will warn those kids before they open the channel and let the water back in the reservoir." Will looked at the laughing boys one more time. Then sadly, he hopped on his bike and started to ride back to the main road. "Come on," he called to Lassie.

The boy rode slowly down the road toward his house with his happy collie running right beside him. Lassie loved running alongside Will when he rode his bicycle. She loved the feeling of the wind as it rushed through her shiny brown and white fur. She loved the feeling of the soft dirt road beneath her paws. Most of all, Lassie loved spending time with Will. It always made her very happy.

But Will was not happy at all. "Of all the times not to have a skateboard," he murmured sadly to Lassie. "I know one thing. When I get a new one, I'm going to take great care of it. And I'm not going to let anyone borrow it, either!"

At the end of the road, Will came upon three bright orange traffic cones that blocked any cars from going down the street toward the reservoir. A sign looped over the center cone warned in big white letters: ROAD TEMPORARILY CLOSED FOR CONSTRUCTION. Will hoped the construction would go on long enough for him to have a chance to try a few skateboard wheelies with the other kids.

Back at the McCullochs's house, Will's fourteen-year-old sister, Megan, was sitting in the living room doing her algebra homework.

She sat sideways in a big, overstuffed easy chair, with her legs stretched over one arm of the chair and her long blonde hair draped over the other arm. Their mother, Dee, was doing some work at her desk. Dee owned a personnel business. She matched up interested workers with companies that could use their services. It was a convenient business because Dee could do most of the work from her desk in the living room of her home. Dee looked over at her daughter from across the room and frowned.

"After about fifteen minutes you might want to shift your legs over to the other side. That way you'll wear out the chair more evenly," Dee teased Megan.

"Good idea," Megan said with a smile, as she played along with her mother's teasing.

"Or possibly, you might even want to sit the regular way. Who knows? It might even be more comfortable."

Megan looked down at her algebra book and groaned. "When you're doing homework," she grumbled, "no way is comfortable."

Dee looked at Megan and shrugged. She was about to go back to work when her husband Chris came storming down the stairs and into the living room.

"I can't believe this telephone bill!" he bellowed, waving the blue and white papers in the air. "Look at all these calls to San Diego!" He held the bill out in front of him and looked down the list of long-distance numbers. "Area code 619 . . . area code 619 . . . 619 . . . 619 . . . !" Annoyed, he handed the bill over to Dee for a look.

Dee scanned the bill for a while and looked over at Megan. "I think most of these were to Megan's friend Becky."

"That's what I was afraid of." Chris sighed.

Megan got up from her chair and walked over to her mother. "Let me see that," she said, taking the bill. "Yep, that's Becky's number all right." Megan wasn't the least bit surprised. She knew that most of the calls would be to her old friend from San Diego. The McCullochs had moved north to suburban Glen Ridge, California, from San Diego only a few months ago and Megan was still attached to her friends in the old neighborhood. Not that she hadn't made lots of friends in Glen Ridge. She had met a lot of people by getting involved in various school activities like the photography club. She had even become the mascot for the Glen Ridge High School cheerleaders! But no matter how many friends Megan made in suburban Glen Ridge, she was still attached to her old city pals.

"This is terrible," Chris groaned as he slumped into a chair and looked once again at the costly phone bill.

"Sweetheart, don't worry," Dee consoled him. "Megan and I will talk about this."

"No, I mean I feel terrible," Chris said without looking up.

Megan giggled. "You're supposed to. That's what dads do. They get upset about phone bills." She laughed.

Chris took a deep breath. "What I am saying is that it's all my fault. If I hadn't moved my construction business out of San Diego and dragged us up here to Glen Ridge . . ."

". . . to live with a bunch of hicks," Megan interrupted him.

"Megan!" Dee scolded. She really got annoyed when Megan talked like a city snob.

"Come on, Mom," Megan teased. "Dad doesn't feel guilty all that often. You've got to take advantage of it when you can."

But Chris didn't see any humor in the situation at all. He looked at Dee through guilt-ridden eyes. "Don't you see what I've done?" he asked his wife. "In order to have any friends, my daughter is forced to live in the past."

"Look, Will has already made friends here. For that matter, so has Megan." Dee shot her daughter an aggravated glance. "That phone is always ringing for you," she said to Megan.

Before Megan could respond, Will came

slumping into the living room with Lassie padding close behind.

"Hi, Will," Chris said glumly from his chair.

"Hi," Will mumbled. "You are looking at a man with a problem."

"So are you," Chris replied good-naturedly.

"You know that little road that runs next to the reservoir?" Will continued, ignoring his father's comment. "Well, it's closed for construction. Some of the kids have set up the coolest skateboard ramp. It's the perfect place—no cars!"

Dee grew concerned. "Are you sure you are ready for a ramp?" she asked. "It's been a while since I've seen you on your skateboard."

"What skateboard?" Will harrumphed. "I lent mine to Petey Morhead and he left it in his driveway . . . That's my problem. Petey's dad accidentally backed his car over it!"

Chris choked back a laugh. "I trust nobody was on it at the time?" He smiled.

"Dad this is serious! I need a skateboard now! That road could be reopened any day."

"I doubt it," Chris assured him. "I think that street will probably be ripped up for weeks."

But Will wouldn't be consoled. "Do you realize Tim Milford and I are the only two boys in class without skateboards?"

Dee had had just about enough of Will's complaining. "Will, please. Your father can't take any more guilt," she said sternly.

Megan looked up from her algebra homework. "Will, what are you talking about?" she asked. "Tim Milford has a skateboard. I've seen him on it."

"Not lately," Will explained. "His parents grounded him because of his Social Studies grades." Will smiled suddenly. He had a great idea. After a beat he added, "Hey! Knowing Milford, it'll be forever before he gets that grade up. Maybe I can borrow his skateboard."

Dee walked back over to her desk and picked up a pencil. "Problem solved," she said as she looked back down at her paperwork.

"I'll ask him tomorrow after school," Will said gleefully.

"Speaking of Social Studies," Chris remarked, knowing full well he had interrupted his son. "That paper on the Egyptian pyramids is due on the eighteenth, isn't it? That's just three days away."

Will looked at the floor. "I'm basically finished," he said matter-of-factly.

"Basically?" Chris questioned him.

"I just have a few odds and ends to clear up."

"Maybe you could start working on some of

those 'odds and ends' right now," Chris suggested without really giving Will any choice.

Will was about to argue, but one look at his father's face made him change his mind. With a sigh, Will got up and walked to the stairs that led to his room, with Lassie following close behind.

CHAPTER
2

The very next day, as soon as the three-thirty school bell rang, Will ran outside to catch Tim Milford in the school playground before he headed home. Will wanted to ask Tim to loan him his skateboard for a while. As Will crossed the playground to catch up with Tim, visions of homemade pipe ramps and airborne skateboard maneuvers raced through his brain. Finally Will caught up to Tim and his pal Josh on the street that led to the school.

"Hey, Milford! Wait up!" Will called through breathless gasps. Tim and Josh stopped midstep and turned to wait for Will.

"So, Milford," Will asked hesitantly, "you still grounded because of your Social Studies exam?"

Tim kicked at the ground with the toe of his

black canvas high-top sneaker. "Yeah," he answered defensively. "Why?"

"I was just wondering, well . . . uh . . . I mean, since you can't use it or anything, you think maybe I could borrow your skateboard for a little bit?" Will asked, trying not to sound too eager.

"I don't know," Tim said. "I've put a lot of money into this board. New trucks, new rails, grip tape . . ."

Will got very excited. "Oh, man! New trucks and rails!" he interrupted, shouting.

Josh patted Tim on the shoulder. "Why not loan it to him? Staring at the board in your room and not being able to use it is driving you bonkers anyway."

Will shot Josh a grateful glance.

"That's true," Tim began, "but . . ."

Will didn't let him finish. "Great! So you'll do it?" Will squealed, slapping Tim on the back. Will jumped up and down with delight. In his excitement, Will dropped his notebook. His papers went flying all over the place. Tim and Josh bent down to help Will pick them up.

"Hey, look at this," Tim said to Josh, holding up a folder of papers. "This isn't due until October eighteenth! Today's only the sixteenth!

Leave it to a brain like McCulloch to have his Egyptian pyramids paper done two days early."

Will could feel his face burning red with embarrassment. "I guess Social Studies just comes easily to me." He shrugged.

"Come on," Josh urged Tim. "We've got to get going."

Tim ignored Josh. "Hold on a second," he said turning to Will. "You want to borrow my skateboard, right?" Tim asked.

Will nodded, confused.

"Okay, I'll make you a deal," Tim explained. "I'll lend you my skateboard for a whole week and in return you write my Social Studies paper for me."

Will looked stunned. He hadn't planned on having to trade anything for the skateboard—especially not a homework assignment!

"Gee, I don't know," Will began.

"For a smart guy like you, McCulloch, a few pages on the pyramids is nothing," Tim said, smiling.

"Yeah . . . but . . ."

"Okay, fine," Tim said, bluffing. "It was just an idea. Let's go Josh . . ."

Once again Will had visions of the closed off road, the skateboard ramp, and the other kids riding along the reservoir. He just had to have that skateboard!

"Okay, I'll do it," Will said quickly as he grabbed Tim's shoulder to stop him from leaving.

"Great!" Tim smiled. He put out his hand and Will took it. The two boys shook solemnly on the deal.

"Remember who you're writing it for. Better throw in a lot of mistakes to make it look real." Josh laughed. Tim gave his pal a dirty look.

"You bring in my paper tomorrow and I'll give you the skateboard," Tim said over his shoulder as he and Josh left to walk home.

"You bet!" Will shouted after him as he ran home to get started.

That night, right after supper, Will raced up to his room and turned on his computer to write Tim's Social Studies paper. Lassie sat by the side of Will's chair watching him curiously.

The collie was very disappointed. Usually right after dinner, Will would play with Lassie for an hour or two. The two pals would wrestle on the living room floor, or play fetch out in the backyard, or just sit quietly watching TV while Will brushed Lassie's thick, gleaming, brown and white coat with a bristly wire dog brush.

But tonight, Will hadn't taken any time to play with Lassie at all. He had run up to his room to write this paper. No one else in the family had noticed it, but Will seemed just a little nervous about this paper. Lassie was very sensitive to Will's behavior, and she could sense that deep down the boy was uncomfortable with what he was doing. Will could fool anyone but Lassie. Of course, Lassie couldn't know that Will was writing a paper for someone else, but she could sense that whatever Will was doing, it was wrong.

Will opened the encyclopedia to "Egypt" and started to type. "The . . . pyramids . . . of . . . Egypt . . . evolved in the . . . fourth dynasty . . ." he said softly to himself as he typed.

Lassie used her teeth to pick up a small, red rubber ball from under Will's bed. She carried the ball in her mouth until she reached the desk. Then, without a sound, Lassie dropped the ball on Will's desk. With a quick extra motion, Lassie used her long pointed nose to shut the encyclopedia. She wanted to play!

Will steadied the ball on the desk right next to his computer. "Hey, come on," he scolded Lassie. "I've got to get this done. Now don't bug me!"

Will flipped the pages of the encyclopedia until he found his place. Then he laid the book out flat and began typing again. "Each . . . monarch . . . constructed . . . his own pyramid . . ." he typed, "to preserve . . . his mummified . . . body . . . for eternity . . ."

Will didn't turn around, but he could still feel Lassie's icy stare on his back. Finally, he turned in his chair to answer her stern look.

"Look, Lassie," he explained, "this isn't really cheating. It's just . . . just helping a friend."

Lassie held her stare. Something in Will's tone of voice told her that he didn't really believe what he was telling her.

"See, cheating would be if I was having Tim write the paper for me. But since I'm doing it for him . . . it's just a favor."

Lassie shook her head and barked sternly at Will.

"Okay, I'm getting a skateboard out of it . . . But it's only for a week."

Will turned back to his computer. But before he could type one word, Lassie padded over to the computer and put her paws on the desk next to Will. Standing only on her hind legs, Lassie reached up with her paw to bat the red ball from the desk. When she moved, the collie hit the keyboard with her paw.

Will watched in shock as the computer screen went blank. "Lassie!" he shouted in panic as he frantically started hitting the keys on the keyboard, trying to retrieve Tim's report.

"You wiped out my whole report!" he

shouted at the dog. Frustrated, Will got up and took Lassie by the collar. "That's it!" he yelled. "You are out of here!" Then he dragged her down the stairs to the family room.

"Effective immediately," Will announced to his parents, "my room is off limits to Lassie!"

Dee looked up questioningly from her desk. "Off limits?" she asked.

"She just hit my computer and lost my . . . homework," Will explained, stumbling just slightly over the last word.

"Bad dog!" Dee scolded Lassie.

The collie looked up at Will through sad, slanted eyes for a reprieve. But Will avoided her eyes. "Now I'm going to have to start all over again," was all he said.

"Well, don't worry, we won't let her near your room," Chris said. "Lassie, come. Sit," he ordered the dog.

Ever obedient, Lassie moped over to the couch and sat at Chris's feet. She watched with disappointment as Will dashed out of the family room and back up the stairs to his room.

Megan passed her younger brother on the stairs on her way into the family room. "If one of you goes out tonight, could you mail this for me?" she asked her parents as she entered the room, waving a lavender envelope in the air.

"Sure." Chris smiled, taking the envelope from her.

"I want to be sure Becky gets it right away," she said.

Chris looked curiously at the envelope. "There's no stamp on here," he observed.

Megan smiled proudly. "I know. That way we save on the phone bill and on the price of a stamp," she explained. "Becky did it on her letter to me, too. I put her name and address on the back and mine on the front. Then when the post office stamps it 'Insufficient Postage—Return to Sender,' it'll go right to Becky."

Chris shook his head in disbelief. "Megan," he said, "this is crazy—not to mention probably illegal."

"What happens if it comes back to you?" Dee asked. "After all, your zip code is closer."

"I'm desperate to hear from someone from San Diego. I'll read it anyhow," Megan said grinning.

"Forget it." Chris was not amused. "Go put a stamp on it," he said, handing the envelope back to Megan.

Chris's sad eyes followed his daughter as she left the room. Then he sat down on the couch and looked at Dee. "Megan's right about one thing, though." He sighed.

"What's that?"

"I have made her a desperate woman. I know this just sounds like a case of mover's remorse, but I can't help feeling that if we hadn't moved up here, away from her old friends, she'd be hanging out at the mall in San Diego with Becky and her other old friends right now . . ."

Dee smiled gently and moved over to the couch to cuddle up close to her husband. "You're just being hard on yourself. Megan could be hanging out at the Glen Ridge Mall right now with any one of her new friends if she really wanted to."

"Maybe," Chris murmured, unconvinced.

CHAPTER
3

The following day, Will had a tough time paying attention in school. Every time he opened his looseleaf notebook to take notes on the lifestyles of the ancient Egyptians, he found himself doodling pictures of skateboards instead of pyramids. More than once he caught himself staring out the window, daydreaming about doing axle stalls on Tim's skateboard.

Finally school let out. Will met up with Tim and Josh on the same street they'd been on the afternoon before. Will peeked around to make sure no one was watching them or listening in on their conversation. When he was sure the coast was clear, he pulled a red folder holding six white pieces of computer paper out of his notebook and handed it to Tim.

"There you go," Will said proudly. "Six

solid pages, double spaced. I even threw in a run-on sentence or two, plus a couple of spelling errors to make it look good."

Tim flipped through the pages absentmindedly. "I'll take your word for it," he said. "I can't read this stuff."

Josh reached over and closed the folder. "He's an A student. It's got to be good," Josh assured Tim impatiently. "Just give him the board and let's get out of here!"

Tim nodded in agreement. "You wouldn't happen to know anything about ninth grade Spanish, would you?" he asked Will.

Will eyed the skateboard hungrily. He was starting to get annoyed. What did Tim want from him now?"

"Spanish? Afraid not," Will said quickly, staring at the neon green board tucked under Tim's right arm.

"If my brother doesn't get his grade up to a D he's going to be kicked off the Junior Varsity football team," Tim explained.

Will's eyes grew bright. "Oh, sure, your brother is Steve Milford, the star wide receiver on the Glen Ridge High Junior Varsity team," Will said enviously. It must be really neat to have a star football player for an older brother, instead of a sister who liked taking pictures all the time, Will thought.

"With a one point three grade point average," Tim said and laughed, jabbing Josh in the ribs. Will didn't see what was so funny. A one point three grade point average meant that Steve Milford got almost straight Ds on his report card!

"Have Steve call my sister, Megan. She's a wiz in Spanish. She might be able to find a few minutes to help him," Will said helpfully.

"Great!" Tim smiled. "Here's my board," he said, handing Will the green neon skateboard. "Take care of it."

Will reached for the board greedily, unable to disguise how thrilled he was at getting his hands on such a terrific skateboard. "Thanks. I'll have it back in one week," he promised breathlessly. Then, too excited to stand around talking anymore, Will charged off toward his house to change into his old jeans.

"Later maybe we can make a deal for you to do my science project!" Tim called after Will.

Josh looked at Tim and shook his head. "By the way," he asked, "did you remember to get that loose wheel fixed before you gave the board to Will?"

Tim opened his eyes wide and shook his head. "Oops, forgot," he said. Tim watched Josh shake his head again. "I had that dumb Social Studies paper on my mind," he tried to excuse himself, "and, well, it's no big deal. Will's just a little guy. It's not like he's going to shred the reservoir or anything."

"I guess he'll be fine," Josh said, shrugging his shoulders.

As soon as he got home, Will made his usual stop into the kitchen for a few double chocolate chip cookies and a glass of milk. Lassie was so excited to see him that she jumped up high on her hind legs and licked Will right on the nose. Then she followed him around the kitchen, her tail wagging wildly all the way, and watched hungrily as the boy reached into the box for his cookies.

"You want one, too?" Will asked Lassie, pointing to his cookies.

As her answer, Lassie wagged her tail even harder. Will smiled at her, then reached under the sink and pulled out a box of tan-colored, bone-shaped doggie biscuits. "This bone's yours." He laughed as he handed her the dog cookie. When his glass was drained and his cookies were eaten, Will went up the stairs to change his clothes. His faithful collie followed close behind him.

Downstairs in the family room, Megan was talking on the phone. She was in her usual sideways position in the overstuffed easy chair, with a textbook open in her lap and the phone receiver tucked tight between her right ear and her right shoulder.

"Yo voy, tú vas, él o ella va, nosotros vamos, ustedes van, ellas o ellos van," she said into the receiver.

Chris and Dee walked into the room as she was speaking. They watched as Megan listened to the party on the other end of the phone, smiled brightly, and then said, "Great. See you then. Bye!"

Chris laughed as his daughter hung up the phone. "Megan, you don't have to talk to your friends in code," he teased, knowing full well she was speaking in Spanish.

"Just practicing Spanish verbs with Steve Milford," Megan explained. "Dad, I have to make one more call to San Diego," she added sweetly.

"No more return-to-sender letters?" Chris teased.

"This is too important for a letter. I want to tell Becky all about Steve. I promised to study with him Saturday. If he doesn't get his Spanish grade up, he's off the team. And he's the star player!" Megan spouted out, all in one breath.

"But isn't Steve Milford just another 'hick'?" Dee asked with a sarcastic smirk. "What about all your city friends in San Diego?"

"Oh, Becky's still my best friend, that's why I want to call her," Megan assured her mother. "But San Diego is yesterday. After all, I live in Glen Ridge now. I should be hanging out with my friends from here."

Dee put her arm around Chris's waist as they watched Megan run upstairs to make her phone call in private.

"If Steve Milford stays on the team, they should give Megan a Junior Varsity letter," Dee said, giggling.

Just then Will came running down the steps, skateboard in hand. "I'm off," he called to his parents. "Refer all my calls to the skateboard ramp."

Before Will could get out the door, Lassie came running up beside him, holding his helmet by the strap between her teeth. Will tried to wave the dog away, but she plopped the helmet down on the floor right in front of him.

Dee walked over and petted the collie gratefully along her broad golden brown back. "Look at that. Skateboard helmet and pads. You never forget anything. Good girl," Dee complimented her.

Will was less than pleased. He was hoping to sneak out without his helmet and pads. After all, what would a cool big kid like Hacksaw think of a helmet and pads?

"Yeah, good going," Will said to Lassie in a most unconvincing manner. With a resigned sigh, Will bent down and picked up the helmet and pads.

"Will, when you get home, there may not be anyone here, so take your keys," Dee told him. "Dad and I are going to pick up the 4×4 in the shop, and we're dropping Megan off at the library."

"No problem," Will answered. Then he rushed out the door before anything or anyone else could stop him.

As soon as he and Lassie were outside, Will stopped to scold Lassie. "First you wipe out my report on the computer, and now this," he said angrily, holding up the helmet. "Who's side are you on, anyhow?"

Lassie whined a quiet sigh and rubbed up against Will's leg lovingly to show that she was always on his side, no matter what. She just wanted to make sure he was safe! Will sighed and put on his helmet and pads. When he was finished, he hooked Lassie's long leather leash up to her collar. Then, holding on to Lassie's leash, Will hopped on the skateboard and let the dog tow him through the streets to the reservoir.

Finally, the boy and his dog reached the blocked off street. Lassie led Will between two of the three rubber orange cones that blocked off the street and over to the ramp. Will watched excitedly as some of the boys did Japan Airs, Mc-Twists, and Drop Ins in the air. Will felt a little better about his safety equipment when he saw that all the boys—except for Hacksaw—were wearing their helmets and kneepads. He might not look as cool as Hacksaw, but at least he didn't look like a weirdo.

Hacksaw looked over and spotted Will and Lassie. "Well, look who's here," he called in a taunting voice. "Come on! Take a shot!"

Will jumped off the skateboard, flipped it up in the air with his toe and caught it expertly with his right hand. "You got it!" he called as he ran down the street and over to the ramp.

When he was a few feet from the ramp, Will hopped on the skateboard and drove for the ramp. He could feel his excitement growing as he heard the skateboard slam onto the home-made ramp and then sail off it, flying in the air for just a second. Before he knew it, Will landed back on the ground again with a slam as the wheels of the skateboard smacked the pavement.

"All right, McCulloch!" one of the boys from Will's class at school complimented him on his jump.

"Yeah, good one!" called another.

Hacksaw wasn't the least bit pleased with

all the attention Will was getting. He was used to having all the compliments for himself. "Not bad," he said matter-of-factly. "But you didn't get enough air into it."

Lassie watched Will nervously from the sidelines. She didn't like the way the back wheel on the borrowed skateboard seemed to wobble back and forth. If the wheel dropped off the board in midflight, Will could slip from the board and really hurt himself.

"Ruff! Ruff!" Lassie tried to bark a warning to Will. But the boy was having too much fun to pay any attention to the message.

CHAPTER
4

One by one, the boys took turns taking off from the ramp and trying new aerial stunts. Hacksaw showed off for the crowd by taking off from the ramp and landing with one leg bent low to the ground and the other extended in a perfect "shoot the duck" style.

The older boy smirked slightly as the other boys cheered him on. But he turned and faced the ramp as Will raced toward it. Hacksaw stared daringly at Will as if to say, "Top that— I dare you!"

Will tried to keep his concentration on his skateboard, although it was hard for him to take his eyes off Hacksaw's menacing scowl. Will could feel the pressure in the air. All eyes were on him as he took off from the ramp. He was so tense, he barely felt the back wheel of the board shake beneath him. He closed his eyes tight as the board smashed into the ground with a powerful impact. Then, without taking a single breath, Will threw up his arms, jumped off his skateboard, turned in the air, and landed back on his board again. Will took a huge breath of relief as his board skidded to a stop. He'd done a perfect spinner!

"Whew!"

"Nice one, McCulloch!"

"Way to go, McCulloch!"

All at once the other boys were surrounding Will, patting him on the back in congratulations! Looking at the scene, Hacksaw could feel the anger and jealousy race through his body.

"Yeah, well watch this," he called to the crowd.

"Sorry, Hacksaw, I gotta get going," Timmy Mullholland said.

"Yeah, me, too," Joey Smith announced.

It was getting dark. Now that it was already October, 17th, the sun was beginning to set much earlier, limiting the amount of time the boys had to play. Many of the boys had to go home for dinner. Eventually it was only Will and Hacksaw alone by the ramp.

"I get the feeling you think you're pretty hot on that skateboard," Hacksaw said challengingly to Will.

"Not really," Will replied modestly.

"Well, maybe you wouldn't feel so secure on that board if you weren't wearing all that wimpy crash clothing," Hacksaw teased.

Will knew he shouldn't take off his helmet and pads. But he just couldn't let Hacksaw think he was a baby. Slowly, Will unfastened his knee-pads.

"Actually, this stuff does sort of get in my way," he said in his most matter-of-fact voice.

Lassie had been watching this whole scene from a distance. After Will had ignored her warning, she'd kept quiet. But this was too much! It was too dangerous for Will to be skating without his safety equipment! Lassie loved Will more than anything in the world. She felt it was her duty to protect him. After all, Will was Lassie's best friend.

"RUFF! RUFF!" Lassie called frantically to Will.

"Quiet!" Hacksaw shouted to Lassie.

Will glared at Hacksaw. Who did this kid think he was, yelling at Lassie like that? Well, Will would show him who was boss! Angrily, Will threw his helmet to the ground.

Laughing, Hacksaw raced up to the ramp, and in seconds exploded in the air, landing with one leg slightly bent on the board and the other straight out. Hacksaw smiled triumphantly as his board tipped backward in a perfect one-foot nose wheelie.

"Bet you can't do that," Hacksaw snarled. Will got very tense. He had never tried landing on one foot before.

"RUFF RUFF!" Lassie barked again.

"Get out of here, you," Hacksaw shouted at Lassie.

That was all it took to get Will going. He would show this bully a thing or two! He raced to the ramp. As he flew through the air, Will was sure his heart had stopped beating. But when he landed on the ground, his working leg was bent slightly, his other leg was pointed out, and his board miraculously tilted backward. He had done it! Maybe his wheelie didn't have the same style as Hacksaw's, but it was certainly okay!

"Ah, this is too easy," Hacksaw said. "Come on. Let's take on that reservoir!"

As Hacksaw moved up the hill he motioned for Will to follow him. Will followed Hacksaw without looking at Lassie. He couldn't stand to look at Lassie now. He knew the dog disapproved of what he was doing, and if there was one thing he couldn't stand, it was Lassie's disapproval.

Will was so determined to keep up with Hacksaw as he climbed the hill that he didn't even notice the bright orange sign that hung from the chainlink fence. CAUTION: RESERVOIR WILL BE REOPENED OCTOBER 17 the sign warned in bold white letters.

As they climbed higher and higher, Will got nervous. "I really don't think we should go in there," Will said tentatively.

Hacksaw laughed heartily. "Are you kidding? Everybody skateboards in here. It's no big deal—unless, of course, you're chicken . . ."

Will wasn't sure why he needed to prove himself to Hacksaw. He just did. So, reluctantly, Will followed Hacksaw as he climbed over the fence.

Lassie was left outside the fence. She watched nervously as Will followed Hacksaw to a steep part of the reservoir.

"This is a good place . . . I'll let you go first this time," Hacksaw told Will.

Will looked down the slope into the base of the reservoir. He seemed so far from the ground.

"Oh, that's okay," Will said nervously. "You can go first. After all, you're more familiar with—"

Hacksaw was growing impatient. "Hey," he said threateningly, moving closer to Will. "I said, you go first. I went first the last time. Fair is fair!"

Will backed away. "Okay," he said unconvincingly. "Sure . . . fair is . . . fair."

Will made his way to the lip of the reservoir and placed his board in position. He stood perfectly still for a couple of seconds as he set himself evenly on the board.

Will shut his eyes and held his breath. Then, in one swift motion he pushed off with his left leg. The next thing he knew, Will was racing down the reservoir at top speed, the wind blowing through the hair on his now unprotected head. Lassie watched breathlessly as Will reached the bottom of the reservoir and came up the other side doing an almost perfect axle twist.

Hacksaw followed, making the exact same motions as Will. When the two boys met up again, Will said a sincere "Nice going," to the older boy.

Hacksaw muttered an insincere "Thank you."

"Let's try it from over there," Hacksaw said to Will, pointing to an even higher part of the reservoir.

Will looked at the steepness of the slope. He got really scared. "Maybe we should stop now," he said, almost pleadingly. "I think it's starting to get dark."

"I'm not scared of the dark. Are you?" Hacksaw taunted.

"No, but . . ."

"Good," Hacksaw said, ending the discussion. "This time I'll go first."

Lassie watched as the boys moved farther up the hill. The wise collie knew Will was not experienced enough to ride the board from there—especially not with a shaky back wheel. Quickly she ran to the low part of the fence and tried to leap over it. But although she leaped as high as her collie legs would go, Lassie couldn't get enough height to jump over the fence. She was forced to give up. Frantically, Lassie charged up the hill, barking a warning to Will.

When they reached the top, Will looked at Hacksaw. "You sure you want to do this, Hacksaw?" he asked, his voice shaking. "It's pretty steep here."

Hacksaw didn't reply. He just sneered at Will. Then the bully set himself solidly on his board, kicked off, and went speeding down the hill faster than Will had ever seen anyone move on a skateboard. Will watched with genuine admiration as the bigger boy angled down the steep side of the reservoir and banked around the curved corner, picking up just enough momentum to send himself gliding up the adjoining wall. Will was about to applaud when suddenly, Hacksaw lost control of his skateboard. The board slipped out from under him at top speed!

Will ran down the hill toward Hacksaw. Lassie followed his movements from her side of the fence. When Will reached Hacksaw, he noticed a trickle of a tear coming from the boy's eye. Hacksaw was really in pain.

"It's my leg . . ." Hacksaw began, clutching at his calf.

Will wanted to say, "Not bad but you didn't get enough air into it," just as Hacksaw had done to him, but seeing the boy lying there in pain, Will didn't have the heart. Instead, he bent over and looked at Hacksaw's leg. "Okay, just try to take it easy and we'll get you out of here," Will said calmly.

"How? I can't walk," Hacksaw snarled.

Will stopped to think. "Good question," he answered slowly. Will looked up. The sun was setting rapidly. It was getting dark. Before long, the two boys would be stuck all alone in the dark at the bottom of the reservoir!

Lassie was desperate to get to Will. Using her sharp nails to dig, the resourceful collie dug a hole under the fence, deep enough for her to crawl through. Before he knew it, Lassie was at Will's side, offering her assistance.

"Good girl, Lassie." Will smiled, petting her.

"That's all we need," Hacksaw moaned. "A dog."

Will ignored him. "Maybe she can help," Will thought out loud. "Hold on to her collar," he ordered Hacksaw.

"What!" Hacksaw shouted at Will.

"Just hold on to her collar!" Will repeated.

Hacksaw was in no position to argue. He took hold of the collar and, with Lassie pulling and Will pushing, the two tried to roll Hacksaw up the reservoir. They struggled bravely, but the hill was just too steep.

"RUFF! RUFF! RUFF!" Lassie barked her most ferocious warning bark.

"What is it, Lassie?" Will said, alarmed by the severity of her barks. Lassie motioned toward the top of the reservoir with her head.

"Oh, no!" Will cried out in fear. Water was rushing down the side of the reservoir from the flood channel.

"They've opened the flood channel. This place is going to be full of water before we know it!"

CHAPTER
5

"I'll drown!" Hacksaw cried out in a voice filled with fear and desperation. "I can't swim!" The older boy looked at Will through pleading, frightened eyes. "Do something. Get your parents."

His mother's words raced through Will's mind. "When you get home there may not be anyone here . . ."

"They're not home," Will said quickly to Hacksaw.

Hacksaw fidgeted nervously as he watched Will standing quietly and studying the open flood channel. The now vulnerable bully shouted loudly as Will started to walk up the steep slope of the reservoir to the channel.

"Where are you going? Are you going to just leave me here?"

"Stay right here," Will ordered Hacksaw.

Hacksaw looked down at his swollen leg. "Where am I gonna go?" he asked sarcastically.

Will ignored the comment. "Keep an eye on him, Lassie," was all he said before he left.

Left alone together, Lassie and Hacksaw eyed each other with resentment. Neither one was too fond of the other.

Will ran up the side of the reservoir at top speed. He climbed over the fence in one continuous movement. He knew he didn't have much time. Rapidly, Will ran over to the closed-off road and grabbed the makeshift skateboard ramp. The ramp was heavy, and it took more strength than Will ever knew he had to drag it up the hill and over to the spot where the flood gate emptied the gallons of fast flowing water into the reservoir. Will turned the skateboard ramp on its side and shoved it across the spillway so that the water was redirected away from the reservoir and off to the side. Will turned and braced himself against the ramp to make sure that the water wouldn't force itself past the ramp and go rushing into the reservoir.

"Lassie! Here, Lassie!" Will called to his dog from his post at the flood channel.

At the sound of her master's voice, Lassie left Hacksaw's side and went tearing up the side of the reservoir. She climbed through the hole she had dug under the fence, and ran right for Will.

"Good girl," Will said as calmly as he could. Will was having a tough time remaining calm. Despite his efforts, some of the water was spilling into the reservoir, and the water level at the bottom of the reservoir was growing, however slowly.

Hacksaw could feel the water beginning to surround him. He was growing more and more anxious. From where he sat, he could see Will petting Lassie, and whispering something in her soft triangular ear.

"Forget that dog!" He yelled angrily up to Will. "I'm the one who is hurt!"

Will ignored Hacksaw's cruel remarks. Will understood that right now, "that dog" was the only one who could save Hacksaw's life!

"Go, Lassie . . . Go!" Will commanded his dog, pointing in the direction of the main road. "Get help!"

Lassie took off with the force of a rocket! Will followed with his eyes as her brown and white body sped away from him until she was completely out of his sight. Once she was gone, Will focused all of his attention on the petrified boy at the bottom of the reservoir. "Hurry, Lassie! Hurry!" Will prayed silently.

* * *

Lassie was doing her best. Already the dog had run down the closed road, past the three orange traffic cones, and come to a stop at the cross street. Lassie's heart pounded with nerves and hope as her sensitive ears picked up the sound of a car coming toward the crossroad. As the car approached, Lassie jumped up and down, barking frantically in order to get the driver's attention and divert him up the closed road to the reservoir. But all of Lassie's frantic jumping and barking was to no avail. The driver ignored the collie's desperate cries and drove on.

Lassie hadn't considered how difficult it would be to get humans to understand what she wanted them to do. But Lassie wouldn't give up. Within minutes she picked up the sound of a second car coming toward her. With renewed enthusiasm Lassie ran alongside the car, trying to get the driver to follow her to Will. Unfortunately, the driver of the car did not get Lassie's message either, and he drove past, ignoring the barking collie.

Lassie was getting very frustrated. She was about to turn back and join Will when she spotted the three orange traffic cones that blocked off the street. Lassie's ears perked up and her tail wagged ever so slightly as an idea bloomed in her mind. With swift, determined motions Lassie picked up the first of the three cones in her strong jaws and dragged it over to the side of the road behind some shrubbery. One by one she dragged all three cones away from the road and hid them behind the thick shrubs. When the last cone, the one with the ROAD CLOSED warning sign around it, was out of the way, the wise collie stood quietly by the side of the road and waited patiently for the next car to come.

Finally a red convertible came driving into the intersection where Lassie stood watching. The driver, having no idea that he was traveling on a road that was closed for construction, drove unaware up the hill toward the reservoir.

Lassie watched with a sigh of relief as the car traveled in Will's direction. She had found the perfect way to get help. But there wasn't time for Lassie to be proud. Will still needed her help. So, with her collie mouth pulled back in a triumphant smile, Lassie followed the car up the hill toward the reservoir, barking all the way.

"Ruff! Ruff! RUFF!" Lassie's loud barks rang out sharp and loud in the crisp fall air as she alerted Will that a car was on its way. The sound of Lassie's barking caught Will's attention. As he turned his head in the direction of the sound, Will spotted the red convertible coming up the slope.

"Help! Help!" Will called from his post at the flood channel. "Help! Help!"

Lassie wasn't taking any chances that the driver wouldn't hear Will's shouts. The collie bravely ran as fast as she could until she caught up with the convertible. Then, without a thought for her own safety, Lassie jumped right out in front of the car!

SCREEEECH! The driver jammed on the brakes of the car and squealed to a halt—missing the beautiful purebred collie by less than a quarter of an inch!

The driver of the convertible forced open his car door and jumped out to see if the dog was all right. When he did, he spotted Will at the top of the hill, using all his strength to hold the homemade ramp in place.

"What the . . ." the driver began, looking from the boy at the top of the hill to the frantically barking dog and back again.

"Down there, mister," Will called to the man, pointing to Hacksaw, who was by now sitting in a pool of water and crying hysterically in fear for his life.

"Oh my goodness," the driver shouted as he leaped over the chainlink fence and ran to help Hacksaw.

"It's going to be okay," Will called excitedly to Hacksaw. "Lassie got help!"

EPILOGUE

"I know . . . I know . . . when people build a fence around something, it's for a reason," Will repeated the words his father had been saying over and over again for the past hour.

The kind man who had been driving by the reservoir in his red convertible had carefully lifted Hacksaw out of the reservoir and up to safety. Then he had used his car phone to call the hospital and have them send an ambulance to help the boy. After they had carefully placed Hacksaw in the back and put his leg in a splint, the emergency rescue workers had offered Will a chance to ride in the ambulance with them, but they made it clear that Lassie had to follow behind in the red car. As much as he wanted to ride in a speeding ambulance, Will chose to ride along with his heroic and quick-thinking collie.

When Chris arrived at the hospital, he took one look at his son and gave silent prayer of thanks that Will was all right. Chris didn't say a word in the hospital about the incident, nor on the long ride home. But as soon they walked in the front door, Chris had both Will and Lassie take a seat on the living room couch. Only then did Chris begin his lecture on safety, following rules, and reading signs. Will sat quietly on the couch, fidgeting ever so slightly.

"Fences are meant to keep people out—or, in a few cases, keep people in," Chris said, making a small joke. Will wasn't sure whether to laugh or not, so he managed a small smile.

"I knew I shouldn't have gone in there, but Hacksaw kept saying it was okay . . . 'Everybody does it.' "

Chris looked at his son sternly. "Well, you'll just have to decide who you are going to listen to in life . . . Your friends or yourself. It's not an easy choice."

"Especially if you like what your friends are saying better," Will thought out loud.

"And speaking of friends," Chris continued. "You can bet the next time Hacksaw skateboards, he'll wear his helmet and pads—just like you always do."

Will looked at the floor uncomfortably. It didn't seem like a good time to tell his dad that he hadn't been wearing any protective gear either. Lassie looked at Will knowingly; she could tell he was uncomfortable.

"Ruff. Ruff," she barked quietly, urging Will to tell the truth.

"Shhhh..." Will whispered, gently pushing the dog away.

Lassie's barks and Will's motions were not lost on Chris. "Just think, you could be the one at St. John's hospital with the compound fracture of the tibia..." Chris suggested to Will.

Will shuddered at the thought. "Uhhhh," he moaned, thinking of Hacksaw sitting at home with a cast up to his hip.

"... Especially because you had a loose wheel on your skateboard," Chris continued.

"I'm going to tell Tim about that tomorrow at school," Will vowed.

Chris smothered a knowing grin. "It would serve him right if he got a D on that Social Studies paper," Chris said slowly.

Will's eyes opened wide. How did his father find out about that?

"What?" Will gasped.

"Well, the craziest thing happened this afternoon... I sat down at the computer to punch up the plans for that supermarket I'm working on over on Ontario Street," Chris began, noting the guilty look that had become apparent on his son's face. "And, well, let me put it this way . . . I just hope this supermarket doesn't come out looking like an Egyptian pyramid . . . with Tim Milford's name on it!"

"Oh, no," Will moaned.

"Will, we're living in a new age now," Chris said with a half smile. "You're going to have to learn to erase your floppy discs!"

Will shrugged his shoulders and collapsed wearily into the couch. There was no sense trying to deny it—he had been caught on all counts! Even without his father saying it, Will knew it would be a long time before he would be allowed out on a skateboard again. He was sure to be grounded!

Lassie knew it, too. But unlike Will, she was thrilled. Lassie could wrestle with Will, run with Will, play fetch with Will, even watch TV with Will. Just about the only thing she couldn't do with Will was ride his skateboard. Lassie snuggled up beside Will and licked his nose with her rough pink tongue. Then she rolled over and exposed her white chest.

Will smiled as he scratched Lassie's belly. Being grounded wasn't too bad—especially if you lived in the same house with your very best friend!

DANGER ZONE

A Novel by Nancy E. Krulik
Based on the Al Burton Production LASSIE
Adapted from the episode "WATCH YOUR
STEP "
Written by Alan Moskowitz

CHAPTER
1

"Lassie! Fetch!"

Will McCulloch threw the softball high in the air and watched it soar across the open field. It landed with a small plop on the grass that grew around the roots of a sturdy elm tree. The ten-year-old boy waited patiently while his beloved purebred collie, Lassie, chased after the old, yellowed leather softball. The dog looked like a gleaming streak of white and golden brown fur as she ran across the field. When Lassie finally reached the tree, she looked at the ball, picked it up in her mouth, and held it firmly in her mighty jaws as she trotted quickly back to Will. Just as Lassie reached her master, she opened her mouth and proudly dropped the ball right in front of his worn, black, high-top sneakers. Then she looked up at him, wagged her tail in joy, and turned around to face the tree again. It was the fun-loving collie's way of telling Will that she wanted to play some more.

Will picked up the ball and made a face. His softball was wet with the saliva from the collie's mouth, and there were tiny toothmarks in the worn, grass-stained leather. Will tossed the ball in the air, then he caught it smack in the center of the brown leather baseball mitt that covered his left hand. He turned and looked at his fourteen-year-old sister, Megan, who was busy taking pictures with her new 35-millimeter camera. "C'mon Megan," he pleaded. "Play catch with me. I need the practice."

Megan looked up from her camera lens for just a second. "Sorry, Will," she said bluntly. "No time for games. The camera rules!" Then she smiled and snapped a picture of her brother's disappointed face.

"Hey!" he complained. Will hated it when his sister took his picture. And since she was such a photography buff, Meg spent a lot of time taking pictures of the family. Still, Will wanted Megan to play catch with him, so he decided to be a little more tolerant of having his picture taken this time.

"Please, Megan! You throw a lot better than Lassie."

Megan gave an angry sigh and stared at Will.

"Look, I was supposed to be with my photography club at the beach today, but you forgot to give me the message," Megan snapped at her brother.

Will looked down toward the ground and kicked at the pale green grass with the white toe of his sneaker. He couldn't deny that he had forgotten to give his sister the phone message. Still, it wasn't *completely* his fault.

"You get fifteen calls a day! I can't remember them all."

It was true. The McCullochs had moved to Glen Ridge just a few months ago from San Diego, so that the kids' dad, Chris, could build a more successful construction business. Will and Megan's mom, Dee, had her own personnel business. It was her job to find good employees to work for some of the major businesses in town. Dee worked with a lot of people, and that had helped the elder McCullochs make new friends in Glen Ridge. Will had made a few friends, too, mostly with kids he knew from playing on the soccer and baseball teams at school. Still, Will and his parents were pretty lonely. They didn't have nearly as many friends as they had had in San Diego. But Megan had made lots of friends in Glen Ridge. In just a few short months, she had become a star member of the photography club and the mascot of the Glen Ridge High School Cheerleading Squad. Her many friends started calling the McCulloch house the minute they got home from school. Sometimes it seemed like no one else in the house ever got to use the phone. So it was only natural that Will might forget to give Megan one little message.

But Megan wasn't listening to any of Will's excuses. She really would have liked to go to the beach today. "What can I expect from a baby brother whose best friend barks?" she asked sarcastically, tossing her long blonde hair behind her and staring right at Lassie.

Will stopped playing catch and looked at his sister in amazement. He couldn't believe she could be so cruel with her teasing. Not only was she calling him a baby, but Megan was poking fun at his close relationship with Lassie. *Of course* he loved Lassie. She had been a part of his life ever since he could remember. Lassie wasn't just his dog, she was his pal and his protector. Will bent down and petted Lassie.

"That's all right, girl," he said to the collie, stroking the white spot at the top of her long, regal head. "She doesn't mean anything." Lassie snuggled up close to Will and licked his nose with her wet, rough, pink tongue. Will smiled a bit as he wiped the wet dog kiss from his nose.

Megan felt her face get hot and red with embarrassment. To avoid looking at Will, she turned away and started taking more photographs. The truth was, Megan loved Lassie just as much as

Will did, and she hadn't really meant to get her brother so upset. But Megan was very angry and disappointed. And sometimes, when she got that way, she said things she really did not mean. And today was one of those times. After all, because of Will's forgetfulness, instead of taking pictures of the waves, sand castles, and sea gulls, and hanging out with her friends on the beach, Megan was stuck playing on some field with her little brother and the family collie.

Well, at least I'm still taking pictures, Megan thought to herself. And this land *is* awfully pretty.

Megan looked through the lens of her camera at the fresh, flowing stream that looked like a sheet of cool, clear diamonds under the sun's bright glare. The reflections of the trees in the water would make some interesting photographs. There were also plenty of bright, colorful, wildflowers to photograph, not to mention groves of fascinating old, twisted, trees that had been bent into unique shapes by many storms over time. Of course she would never let Will know it, but as soon as Megan had arrived at the field, she had decided that if she had to be stuck with her brother and his dog all day, this was a pretty good place to be stuck.

Megan and Will had driven over to the field early in the morning with their parents in the family's shiny black 4×4. As they had driven up to the land, everyone became overwhelmed by the sheer beauty of the acreage that lay before them. It was hard to believe that such untouched wilderness could be less than one hour from suburban Glen Ridge, with its houses, parking lots, and stores. This field was truly nature at its finest. As soon as Chris had parked the 4×4, Megan had loaded film into her camera and run off to take pictures, Will and Lassie trudging close behind.

The field Megan and Will were playing in was part of four hundred acres of undeveloped land that Arthur Reynolds, an old family friend, had bought from the government. Back in San Diego, Arthur had been in the construction business just like Chris McCulloch. In fact, he had helped get Chris started in the business. Arthur, his wife, Ellen, and their son, Kevin, had moved north to Glen Ridge about two years ago. Now Arthur was a big-time real estate developer, and he was worth millions of dollars!

But he did not forget old friends. As soon as he heard Chris McCulloch had moved to Glen Ridge, Arthur had offered Chris the opportunity of a lifetime! He wanted to hire Chris's construction company to level the land so that it could be developed into a whole community.

"Hi, Mom!" Will shouted over to his mother. His parents were standing outside of a construction trailer across the field.

"Hey, there," his mother called back. "Don't wander away too far," she called. "You either, Megan," she added.

The kids nodded in response and then walked out into the open fields.

"All this acreage is going to be turned into housing," Chris McCulloch said to his wife, pointing to a few spots on the map that lay in front of them. "There will be schools and parks, hospitals and libraries. This job is a builder's dream! Arthur sure has done well since he moved here," he added with more than just a twinge of envy.

Dee smiled and patted her husband's arm encouragingly. "So have you! He's just been here longer." Then she quickly changed the subject. "I can't wait to see Ellen," she said. "It's going to be fun catching up on each other's lives."

"Maybe we should have told the kids to be here with us when Arthur arrives, instead of taking a walk," Chris said nervously. The idea of seeing his friend after so much time made him very anxious. After all, Arthur was a very rich man now. Perhaps he had changed.

Dee understood what her husband was going through. She tried to calm him. "He's your friend, Chris, not some inaccessible robber baron. It will all work out fine," she assured him.

But Chris was not at all sure of that. Already, Arthur had sent his assistant, Larry, to tell Dee and Chris that he would be late for their meeting. An assistant! Chris couldn't believe it!

"Who would have imagined two years ago that Arthur Reynolds would have an assistant!" Chris thought out loud. "That costs a lot of money!"

"The price for success," Dee answered him.

"I'd pay it," Chris said, looking earnestly at his wife.

Dee looked lovingly up at him. She just had to make him see that all the money in the world could not buy what she already had. When she spoke, she chose her words very carefully.

"Look, Chris, I have everything I need. Anything else we get in life—houses, cars, assistants, a bigger business—it's all just gravy."

Chris gave her a tight hug. "Hey, what's wrong with a man wanting to pour a little gravy over his wife?" he kidded her.

Dee burst out laughing. Now that was the Chris she knew and loved! She smiled as she watched him look over the plans one more time before Arthur arrived.

Meanwhile, out in the field, Will was still trying to get his sister to play with him. He felt really bad about forgetting to give her the message about the beach party, and he just wanted her to forgive him.

"Hey, Megan," he called to his sister, who was busy photographing a bright yellow and black sunflower that was growing wild in the field. "How about a picture of Lassie catching the ball?"

But Megan wasn't ready to forgive and forget just yet. "Oh boy," she muttered sarcastically. "You could hang it in your room right next to Spiderman and the 'Inedible' Hulk," she teased. When he was a little boy, Will had had a tough time saying "The Incredible Hulk." It always came out "The Inedible Hulk."

That last teasing jab was more than Will could take! He was sick and tired of Megan treating him like a baby!

"I said I was sorry about the phone message!" he shouted at her angrily. He was so mad his face turned beet red and the purplish blue veins in his neck bulged.

"I know you did," Megan said quietly. She was shocked by her brother's furor.

"So you don't have to tease me," Will said, a little calmer now.

Megan stood straight and tall and looked at her brother. "So tease me back. I can take it," she said, pounding on her chest with her fist as a show of strength.

"That's not fair," Will sulked. "You're better at it than I am."

"Look, Will, it's the survival of the oldest.

Maybe one day Mom'll have another baby and it'll be your turn."

The thought of a new baby in the house gave Will the creeps. "No, thank you," he said, so strongly that he made Megan laugh.

Quietly, the two kids walked up a small hill. Lassie padded slowly behind them, stopping every now and again to dig at the dirt with the sharp nails on her front paws, or to scratch her broad, brown and white back against the bark of a tree.

Eventually, Megan pulled out her camera and started shooting more pictures. Will and Lassie followed behind her, playing fetch with the softball. Just ahead, Megan spied an old tree on a hill beyond the aluminum fence that marked the end of one field and the beginning of the next. Megan was sure it would be just perfect for photographing. She ran at top speed through an open gate in the fence and into the next field.

Will and Lassie hurried to keep up with her. The kids were so busy running, they did not notice the large red metal sign that hung from the swinging gate. In bright white letters, the sign warned:

DANGER! NO TRESPASSING! HAZARDOUS AREA!

CHAPTER
2

"Here comes the picture of the year," Megan screeched excitedly over her shoulder to Will as she darted right over to an oak tree in the middle of the second field. The tree was old and weatherbeaten. Its thick trunk was charcoal gray, and its roots were long and winding, sticking up high above the ground. The branches of the tree were twisted and turned, so that it looked much like one of the old apple trees that came to life in the movie *The Wizard of Oz*. Immediately, Megan balanced herself on the shallow, sloping hill across from the tree and started taking pictures of its green leaves and mighty trunk.

Will followed Megan to the hill, laughing slightly to himself about his sister's enthusiasm over an old tree. Sometimes he could not believe the silly things that made his sister happy. Ordinarily, Lassie would have galloped eagerly beside Will, happy to be out in a wide open space. But curiously, the collie stayed behind, standing completely still, with her hairy triangular ears pointing straight up on the sides of her head. Something about this place made the wise collie very nervous. Collies have sharp ears. They pick up sounds long before their eyes can make out what is creating the sound. Now Lassie's powerful ears were picking up an unfamiliar sound—something like the distant ticking of a clock. Lassie wasn't sure what was making the sound, but she had no interest in finding out what it was, either.

Will turned around and looked at Lassie with surprise. He was shocked to see his usually brave collie acting very nervous. Lassie's head was at attention and her long, thin collie nose was pointing straight out over the field, as if she were trying to pick up some sort of scent. Her tail, which was usually moving back and forth in a brown and white wag of delight, was still and aimed at the ground. Will looked around. He thought that maybe Lassie heard or smelled a rabbit or some other animal in the woods. But Will could see no animals anywhere. Not that that meant anything. Lassie could always spot a rabbit faster than any human. Still, he thought to himself, if Lassie *had* smelled or heard an animal, she would have been off and running after it by now. No, something else was definitely bothering the dog.

"Megan, something's bothering Lassie," Will called to his sister. Then he turned and headed back toward the edge of the fence where his dog was standing.

Megan pulled her camera away from her eye and sighed heavily. She really did not like having her concentration broken when she was in the middle of a good photo shoot.

"Look, Will, you can stay and analyze her if you want," she said in an impatient tone of voice, "but I'm moving closer to get a better shot."

Will looked from his dog to his sister. Megan was already moving farther down the hill toward the roots of the tree. Will looked off in the direction of the trailer. It was out of view now. Despite their promise to their mother, the kids had wandered pretty far from where Chris and Dee were working by the construction trailer. Will would never admit it, but he felt a lot safer being near his sister.

"Lassie, come on," Will called to the collie.

Lassie did not want to move, but she was well trained to always follow any order from a member of the family. Will had commanded her to come and she had to obey. Slowly, with her tail dragging between her legs, Lassie moved away from the

fence and reluctantly trudged off after Will and
Megan.

Back at the construction trailer, Dee and
Chris were beginning to think that Arthur might
never drive up. In fact, they were about to track
down the kids and Lassie in the field and call it
a day. But at that moment, a deluxe, red 4×4 with
custom license plates that said BUILDER pulled up.
A driver in a chauffeur's uniform jumped out of
the driver's seat, ran around to the passenger side
and opened the door. Dee and Chris watched in
amazement as their old pal Arthur got out of the
car.

Dee stifled a giggle when she saw her old
friend. Arthur's shirt and tie seemed really out of
place with the faded white hard hat he wore on
his head. He ran over and shook Chris's hand pow-
erfully and gave Dee a big hug.

"Chris, Dee, welcome to Paradise," he said,
waving his hands out over the land.

"It's really good to see you, Arthur," Dee
smiled. "You look great!"

"Ellen would say I'm too thin," he said, laughing.

"Isn't Ellen with you?" Dee asked in a very
disappointed voice. She really missed her old pal.

"No," Arthur said quickly. Then he changed
the subject. "Hey, where are the kids and Lassie?"

he asked. "I was really looking forward to seeing them."

"They went for a walk," Chris answered. "They'll be back soon. And how's Kevin?" he asked.

Arthur shifted back and forth on his feet uncomfortably. "I'm sorry he's not here for you to see what a great boy he's turning into. Busy kid. No time for his dad."

Dee shot Chris a worried glance. All this work has cost Arthur his family, she seemed to be saying without words to her husband.

Arthur looked at the map of the area that lay across the table next to the trailer. "Let's get down to work," he said cheerfully.

"So the grading and leveling will be needed in these two fields," Chris said, pointing to the two main areas of the land. "Now, what about this area that's surrounded by a fence?" he asked, pointing to the area on the map where, at this very minute, his kids and his dog were wandering.

"The government insists that I personally take care of that area," Arthur explained.

Dee looked over Chris's shoulder at the map. "What exactly did the government use this land for, Arthur?"

Arthur pulled at his collar and looked away. He seemed very nervous and uneasy, as though he were trying to hide something from his friends.

"Oh, anything it wanted," he joked. "You know the government." After a beat he said, "Chris, if this goes right, there'll be plenty more work for you when we start construction. It's your shot at the big time."

Chris smiled and put his hand on his friend's shoulder. "I couldn't ask for a better shot," he said gratefully to Arthur.

Arthur reached out and shook Chris's hand heartily. Then he reached down to his side and pulled up an expensive tan leather briefcase. With his thumbs, he pulled back the catches and the briefcase lid popped open. Quickly, Arthur sorted through some folders, pulled out a pile of papers, and placed them on the table over the map.

"Contracts," he explained. "I believe in a man's word, but my lawyers tell me it never hurts to have his signature as a backup."

Chris nodded and took the papers. He began to flip through the pages of the contract. Then, almost out of nowhere, Arthur's assistant, Larry, came over to the table.

"I'm sorry, Mr. Reynolds," Larry interrupted. "But Pacoma Brick is sending a fax of that proposal over the telephone wire."

Arthur looked apologetically at Dee and Chris. "It never fails," he shrugged. But before he turned and headed into the trailer, Arthur said,

"I'm looking to jump start this project Chris, so do what you can to speed your end up."

As soon as the trailer door shut, Dee whispered to Chris, "At this rate, he'll want you to finish the job before Larry makes lunch."

Chris didn't laugh. He was looking at the deadline dates on the contract. They were very tight. "You just may be right," he said.

"Arthur has really changed."

"Being a millionaire keeps a man busy, honey. That's all," Chris answered her as he continued carefully checking over the contract. Dee peered over his shoulder.

It was about twenty minutes later when Arthur came out of the trailer and stood next to Chris.

"Everything okay, Chris?" he asked, pointing to the pile of contracts.

"Arthur . . . what's this in here about being responsible for any explosives left on the land?" Dee asked.

Arthur looked angrily at Dee and turned to Chris. "Taking in a partner, now, Chris?" he asked, ignoring Dee.

"I thought we were friends," Dee said slowly.

Arthur got red in the face. He had not realized he was being rude by excluding Dee from the conversation.

"Okay," he began. "Up until last year, this

was a military practice range for anything from antitank rounds to experimental artillery shells. There were a lot of duds lying around and a few unexploded shells. So the Environmental Protection Agency insisted that before I could buy the land from the government, I had to clean all the shells out of the fields."

"Well, is it safe now?" Dee asked.

Arthur glanced down at his shoes. "Oh, absolutely," he said. "My explosives experts swept the area last month. It's all strictly according to contract."

Something in his tone of voice made Dee question how true that was. She looked curiously at Arthur and twisted a lock of her short brown hair around her finger.

"Anything else?" Arthur asked quickly, changing the subject once again.

Chris took a deep breath. "I'm afraid there is," he said. "The budget's too small, the schedule's too tight, and I can't afford the penalties if I don't make the schedule."

"Finish on time and you don't have to worry about the penalties," Arthur said gruffly.

"It'll mean cutting corners," Chris argued.

Arthur was becoming frustrated with Chris's need for perfection on the job. He turned to Chris and put his hands squarely on his hips.

"Look Chris," he said sternly. "Let's talk

straight business here. All I ask is that you do the job within the budget I've given. *How* you do it is not my concern."

Dee and Chris stared at Arthur in horror. He *had* really changed. Finally Chris spoke. "That's not the way you taught me to do business," he said to Arthur.

Arthur snickered. "You want to re-pave driveways and build carports for the rest of your life, go ahead. It's your decision. Are you in or out?"

Chris could not believe his ears. Had Arthur really become so cynical? Was this some sort of joke?

While their parents were hammering out the details of the business deal with Arthur Reynolds, Megan and Will were still hanging around by the old tree in the fenced-in field. Lassie was about a half foot away from them, digging furiously in a patch of dirt in the middle of a group of wildflowers. Lassie dug very carefully, being sure that her thick nails did not touch the shiny metal object she had uncovered in the dirt. The piece of metal was about a foot long. It was made of brass and curved in the shape of a long oval. Lassie had no idea what it was, but instinctively, Lassie knew that this odd-looking piece of metal was very dangerous. With a loud *woof* of warning, Lassie backed away from the metal and the flowers. She turned and let out another bark as she walked slowly off into the direction of the fence. She hoped the kids would hear her and follow her lead. Lassie had decided this area was definitely not a safe place to be!

But Megan and Will ignored the dog. Megan was too busy trying to get the best shot possible of the tree, and Will was too busy watching her to pay attention to Lassie. In an attempt to photograph the tree from a new angle, Meg stepped back with her left foot.

"Ruff! Ruff! Ruff! Ruff!" Immediately, Lassie let out a long series of loud low-pitched warning barks. Again Megan ignored her and took another step back. Lassie looked in terror! Megan was about to step on the piece of metal! Lassie took a flying leap in the air and pushed Megan out of the way. Megan let out a scream in shock. Lassie had caught her by surprise! When she finally caught her breath and regained her footing, Megan looked fiercely at Will.

"That dog is mental!" she said pointing to Lassie, who was now circling the piece of brass, eyeing the kids carefully to make sure they stayed away from the metal object. Lassie always made the kids' safety her number one priority.

Will watched his dog with wonder. "Why is she acting like this?" he thought out loud to himself. Megan shrugged her shoulders and bent down to pick up the old softball, which Will had left on the grass by the tree.

"This will keep her busy," Megan suggested to Will. "Lassie, wanna play fetch?" Then she threw the ball hard and fast into the field, in the direction of the tree.

But Lassie had no desire to chase the ball into the field. She watched as the fastball flew through the air and landed with a bounce on the ground.

KABOOM! Suddenly there was a massive explosion! The ground rocked! The sound of the blast destroyed the peaceful quiet that had existed only moments before. The sheer power of the explosion shattered the base of the thick old tree Megan had been photographing!

Lassie let out a series of loud, penetrating barks.

"Megan! Look out!" Will cried.

CHAPTER
3

The explosion that rocked the second field was so powerful that the vibrations shook the ground for miles around. The combined effect of the sudden movement of the land and the ear-shattering blast took Chris, Dee, and Arthur by surprise. It seemed almost like an enemy air raid in a war zone!

"What was that?" Dee shouted over the loud noise of the explosion. Then she realized what had happened. "That was an explosion!" Dee cried in panic as she grabbed hold of Chris's arm and squeezed tightly. Megan, Will, and Lassie were out there in the fields somewhere! What if they had wandered off to that second field, the artillery range Arthur had been telling them about! Dee stared off into the woods with worried eyes.

Chris had the same frightening thought. Instinctively he grabbed Arthur Reynolds by the shoulders and shook him hard. "What's going on, Arthur?" he shouted, looking straight into Arthur's shocked eyes. "Our kids are out there!"

Arthur looked away from his old friend's piercing glare. "I told you, the range was cleared of all hazardous material," he mumbled in a less-than-convincing voice.

"Then what blew up out there?" Chris shouted at Arthur as he shook him fiercely. Chris and Dee were almost wild with fear. Chris had had just about enough of Arthur's obvious half-truths. This was no time for politeness. His kids' safety was at stake. Without waiting for Arthur's response, Chris started giving the orders.

"Arthur, you alert the authorities that there are two kids and a dog out on that artillery range," he demanded.

Arthur knew by the wild look in Chris's eyes that Chris was not going to take "no" for an answer. With a twist of his shoulders, Arthur freed himself from Chris's grip and turned to the trailer.

"Call the army base just outside of Glen Ridge," Arthur told his assistant, Larry, "and let them know what's happening!"

Then, without looking back at Larry, Dee, or Chris, Arthur hopped into the driver's seat of his red 4×4, slammed the door, and started the engine.

"Where are you going?" Larry shouted over the engine's roar.

Arthur did not answer. He just sped off down the road, driving in the exact opposite direction from the route the kids had traveled, leaving a trail of dust behind him.

Dee and Chris weren't waiting around to find out what Arthur was up to. Immediately they jumped into *their* 4×4 and sped off in search of their kids and Lassie! As they drove, they kept their eyes peeled for any sign of a child or a collie.

While Dee frantically scanned the woods, she struggled to keep her imagination from running away with her. She tried desperately to wipe away the mental picture of her children or Lassie lying in pain on the grass. She made a conscious effort not to think about the possibility of any more explosions. Dee took a deep breath. Her only hope was that they would find the kids and Lassie in time!

Out in the second field, Will was staring at his sister through wet eyes. He was petrified. His heart was pounding against his ribs, and no matter how deep a breath he took, he felt as though he could not get enough air to fill his lungs. Crying, Will turned away. He could not stand the sight of Megan lying so still on the ground.

The powerful explosion had cracked the

mighty oak Megan was photographing at its base. When it fell, the tree dropped straight in Megan's direction. Hearing her brother's warning, the girl had tried to run, but she wasn't fast enough. The tree had knocked her to the ground! Now Megan was lying still under the old tree. Her eyes were shut and her breathing was shallow. Will called his sister's name over and over again but Megan couldn't hear him. Please don't die, Megan, Will thought quietly to himself. Please don't die!

Lassie was also afraid for Megan. Like Will, the collie could feel her own heart pounding loudly against her ribs. But unlike Will, Lassie ignored the fear she felt. The brave purebred knew that she had to keep a clear head to save Megan now. Calmly and slowly, Lassie walked over to Megan. Lovingly, Lassie gently licked Megan's eyes and forehead with short, rapid movements of her long, rough pink tongue. After what seemed like hours to Will, even though in reality it was only about two minutes, Megan's eyelids fluttered for a few seconds and then, finally, opened wide. The wise collie's gentle nursing had worked! The first thing Megan saw when she opened her eyes was the inside of Lassie's dark, cavernous collie mouth. Megan rubbed her eyes for a second, and Lassie moved away. It took Megan a moment to remember where she was and who she was with, but eventually she remembered the field, the tree, and that almost ear-shattering noise she had heard before she blacked out.

"Will, what happened?" she asked in a soft, dazed voice.

Will choked back his tears of relief and joy and sat by his sister. He never thought he would be so glad to hear Megan's voice. "I don't know," he answered her. "There was an explosion, and the tree fell . . ."

Megan tried to stand, but the trunk of the tree was resting squarely over her right leg. She shifted her body slightly to try and wriggle the leg out from under the tree, but no matter what position she tried, she could not free herself. Her leg was pinned to the ground under the weight of the tree.

Meg started to panic. Her eyes opened wide and she started to scream. "I'm stuck here! Will, get me out!"

Will jumped to his feet and gripped the tree from underneath. Then, using every muscle in his ten-year-old body, Will tried to lift the oak. Lassie did her best to help Will move the tree. The collie stood sideways next to Will and, planting her white paws firmly into the soft brown soil, pushed all of her weight against the tree. But between them, the boy and the dog did not have the power to move the tree far enough to release its hold on Megan.

"I c . . . ca . . . can't!" Will grunted to Megan as he tried once again to lift the tree. Then he plopped on to the ground, exhausted.

Megan took a deep breath, held it for a second, and then let it out. "Okay," she said slowly. "I gotta calm down. It's not that bad. Nothing's broken." Megan seemed to be trying to convince herself as well as Will. "Will, you go for help," she said calmly.

Without any hesitation, Will stood and took a step in the direction of the trailer. In less than a second, Lassie leaped in front of him and blocked his path.

"Ruff! Ruff!" Lassie barked insistently. Sometimes, when Lassie barked at Will, it almost seemed that the dog was speaking like a human. This was one of those times. Immediately Will understood Lassie was telling him not to move. It was too dangerous. The boy stopped right where he was and watched Lassie carefully, waiting for her to tell him what to do next.

Walking as softly as a cat, Lassie moved less than a few feet away from the fallen tree and lowered her long nose toward the ground. Will followed her and looked down.

"Ah!" he gasped.

"What is it, Will?" Megan called from her spot beneath the tree.

Very slowly, Will moved toward Megan. "An

artillery shell," he said quietly. "There's probably more! I can't go anywhere!"

Will sat next to his sister. His shoulders grew tight with fear and desperation. His head began to throb. What were they going to do?

Lassie sensed that her two beloved friends were very frightened. She wanted very much to comfort them. Lassie did the only thing a caring collie could do to make her master feel better. She lay down next to Will with her paws straight out in front of her. Then, very quietly, she placed her head in his lap and let out a soft, gentle, high-pitched whine.

CHAPTER
4

Will scratched the white spot on the top of Lassie's head and tried to put on a brave smile. "Boy, we were lucky we didn't step on a live artillery shell coming in here," he said to Megan.

Megan looked down at the huge tree that had nailed her leg to the ground. She frowned as she wriggled her foot uncomfortably. Her ankle was beginning to swell. "Somehow, that doesn't make me feel any better," she mumbled sadly.

Will understood how she felt. He was frightened just like Megan, but at least he was free to move. Poor Megan was trapped. She had to be even more scared than Will was! Once again, Will tried to cheer her up.

"At least your camera's okay," he said hopefully.

Megan tried to manage a small grin for Will.

Her little brother really was trying to make her feel better. But the throbbing pain in her leg was getting worse, and she was becoming more and more afraid of being stuck overnight in a field full of live artillery shells. She sighed. "Creating a picture for the newsletter isn't as important as I thought it was," Megan said softly.

Will and Megan sat silently for a while, watching as Lassie sniffed at a large gray rock. Lassie pushed at the rock with her front paws until she forced it out of its spot in the mud. Then her tail began to wag slowly. The kids didn't know it yet, but Lassie had a plan that might save them all! Lassie's head moved up and down ever so slightly as she mapped out her ideas. Lassie knew exactly what needed to be done. Now all she had to do was get Will to do it.

Lassie used her front paws to roll the large gray rock over to Will. Then she looked up at him and barked softly. Finally, she stood tall and turned her head in the direction of the fence.

Will looked at Lassie in frustrated amazement. He could not believe what Lassie was doing. How could she even think of playing fetch at a time like this!

"Not now, Lassie," he said angrily.

But Will had misunderstood Lassie's signals. Lassie knew that this was a serious matter and no time for games. She wasn't trying to play fetch, she was just trying to tell Will about her plan.

Now another dog might have given up at that point and taken Will's "not now" for an answer. But Lassie was not just any dog. Lassie never gave up! She just had to make Will understand that she had a plan to get help. So she used her nose to nudge the rock even closer to Will. Then she let out a slightly stronger bark.

Will looked from Lassie to the rock and back again. Slowly he began to smile. Lassie wagged her tail in response. He understood!

"Woof!" Lassie yelped happily.

"Hey, I got an idea," Will said to Megan as he stood up and picked up the rock.

"What are you going to do?" Megan asked.

"Lassie and I are going to make a safe path out of here. Stay down," he told her.

Megan let out a little giggle. Stay down! She was trapped under a tree! What else could she do?

Will stood far from an artillery shell. Using the baseball throwing skills he had learned as a pitcher in Little League, he aimed the rock right for the nearest artillery shell and threw. Smack! The rock landed right on the shell. Will held his breath, waiting. Nothing happened.

"Whew!" Will let out his breath. "A dud," he called to Megan. Will walked over to the dud.

Lassie trailed close behind the boy. The collie was proud of Will. He was being very brave.

Will picked up another rock. He watched as Lassie gently stepped up on the next slope, searching for more shells that lay on the path that led to the fence. The collie sniffed at the ground for a while until she found what she was looking for. Then, very, very carefully, being sure not to actually touch the shell, Lassie dug through the mud until the shiny brass shell casing was exposed to the sun. Then she ran back to Will, who was standing at a safe distance.

Once again, Will took aim and threw the rock in the direction of the shell. Megan, Will, and Lassie watched as the rock soared through the air and landed right on the metal casing of the shell.

BOOM!

"Ahhh!" Megan let out a scream as the shell exploded in the air. This time it was a live one!

Eventually, the dirt stopped flying and the ground seemed still. Will finally got enough nerve up to bravely step in the direction of the exploded shell.

KABOOM! There was a second explosion from the shell. It was much more powerful than the first. A gray cloud of dust and smoke filled the air, temporarily blinding Megan and Lassie.

"Will!" Megan shouted frantically into the floating dust.

"Ruff! Ruff! Ruff!" Lassie barked.

When the smoke and dust finally settled, Megan could see Will. He had been knocked down by the power of the second, stronger blast. He was lying very still on the ground. Megan's heart skipped a beat. If he was hurt, she would never forgive herself! But Megan gave a huge sigh of relief when she saw her brother stand up slowly and dust himself off. A trickle of blood ran down his arm from a small scratch. He was also going to have one nasty black eye from where a piece of flying rock smacked him, but for the most part, Will was okay!

"Will, forget it," Megan called to him. "Don't throw any more rocks. It's too dangerous!"

Lassie was on her way over to help Will when she stopped in mid trot. The collie held her head high on her neck and pointed her ears upward. She heard something she didn't like. A whirring sound was coming from a pile of dirt that lay a few feet behind the tree that had captured Megan. Lassie crept in the direction of the sound. Will followed her.

Using her acute senses of hearing and smell, Lassie finally found the source of the noise. There, partially hidden in a mound of dirt was an artillery shell. The shell was much larger than any of the others the kids had seen. And this one was making noise! Will took one look at the long, shining metal object that sat in the nest of dirt, and jumped away in fear!

"Oh no!" he cried.

His panicked reaction frightened Megan. "Will, what is it?" she cried, her voice shaking feebly.

"Another shell. A big one! And it's still alive!"

Will looked down at the two-foot long piece of metal and tried not to cry. The whirring sound that was coming from inside the shell was growing louder and louder by the second. Will covered his ears to block it out. He wanted to run to be near Megan, but he was frozen with fear. After all, if he made one wrong move, the shell could explode!

This was the absolute worst mess the McCulloch kids had ever gotten into. If they didn't get out of the field soon, they would be blown to bits!

Megan was shaking. "We've got to get help."

"I can go up the slope . . ." Will said tentatively.

"Oh, no, you don't," Megan stopped him. "The field is too dangerous."

Will moved away from the shell and sat down crosslegged on the ground. He put his head to his knees, hiding his eyes. He didn't want Megan to see that he was crying.

Lassie stepped up close to Will and licked the tears from his face. Then she turned and ran a few steps up the slope. The brave collie was telling

Will that she was going up the slope and across the field to get help.

Will reached over and grabbed Lassie by the collar. "No, Lassie," he cried. "It's too dangerous."

"Ruff! Ruff!" Lassie barked as she tried to yank herself free from his grip.

"Will, let her go. She can sense where things are," Megan explained. "And she may be our only hope," she added in a frightened whisper.

Will felt a lump in his throat. He didn't want Lassie to risk her life for him. But Megan was right. What choice did they have?

The boy grabbed his collie and hugged her tightly, plunging his chubby fingers deep into her thick fur. This time he didn't care if Megan saw him crying. The tears were streaming shamelessly down his cheeks. It took all of his strength for Will to give Lassie a final order.

"Go!" he said simply, opening his arms and setting the collie free.

Without looking back, Lassie trotted steadily up the slope, keeping her ears, nose, and eyes on guard for the slightest sign of a live shell. She moved quickly, but cautiously, across the green field. Every now and again she stopped to sniff at the muddy earth, looking for potential danger spots. Any shell could be alive. At the slightest glimpse of shiny metal, Lassie would sashay carefully around the area. She was taking no chances.

Finally, Lassie reached the fence that blocked her from the main road. She tried to go out through the same gate she and the kids had gone through to get into the field, but some workers had locked it shut—not knowing that two kids and a dog were trapped in the mine field. Lassie would have to break down the fence! Using all her might, Lassie plunged all eighty pounds of her long, lean body into the sturdy aluminum fence. But it was no use. The fence didn't even budge.

Lassie ran at top speed along the length of the fence, looking for a way out. But the fence was ten feet high, and built solidly into the ground. There was no way she could crawl under or climb over it.

Finally, Lassie spied a tall tree growing high above the fence. Taking a running start, the collie used her tight, muscular legs to leap so high she was almost flying. She landed just as she had planned—on the lowest branch of the tree. Then, digging her nails into the bark of the tree for safety, Lassie used her strong jaws to help pull herself up on to the next branch.

It was not easy, but in almost no time at all, the brave collie had reached the top branch of the tree. Looking down, Lassie had a moment of fear. It was a very far drop to the ground. For a second, Lassie wanted to turn and climb back down. But then she thought of Will and Megan trapped in the field all alone. Lassie knew she couldn't let anything stop her now. With a small bark, Lassie set herself, bent her legs, and jumped right over the fence.

Lassie reached the ground outside the fence with a thud. She had landed lopsided and her full weight had pounded onto her right back paw. The pain in the leg was extraordinary. The poor dog gave a sharp cry, then let herself collapse in a heap and curled up for just a second. Finally she stood, being careful to keep all her weight balanced on her three good legs and off of her injured hind leg. Once she had balanced herself, Lassie turned and hobbled down the road in the direction of the trailer.

Lassie had been traveling less than a minute when she heard the familiar purr of a 4×4 car engine. Lassie let out a yelp of joy. Maybe it was Chris and Dee!

But as the car came into sight, Lassie became disappointed. This wasn't the McCulloch's car. This was a different car altogether!

RUFF! Lassie let out a growl as she jumped out of the way of the speeding car. The red car stopped short on the road, just narrowly missing the brave collie. The driver looked out of his window to make sure the animal was safe. When Lassie saw the driver's face she opened her mouth so wide it almost seemed she was smiling. She recognized this man! It was Arthur Reynolds! She had known him since she was a pup back in San Diego!

"Lassie, old girl! Am I glad to see you," Arthur smiled as he reached across the front seat to open the door on the passenger side. Lassie wasted no time jumping up onto the front seat and resting her front paws on the dashboard. She looked at Arthur with grateful eyes. Arthur would help Megan and Will, Lassie was sure of it!

Arthur put the 4×4 in gear and started to drive. But to Lassie's horror, instead of driving straight in the direction of the field, Arthur made a U-turn in the middle of the road and started to drive away from the kids.

"Ruff! Ruff! Ruff!" Lassie tried desperately to signal Arthur to turn around, to tell him he was going the wrong way! But Arthur ignored the collie's loud, insistent barks and kept driving.

CHAPTER
5

The sun was going down at a very rapid pace. The red-orange glow was barely visible behind the mountains now. If the kids did not get out soon, it would be too dark in the unlit field for anyone to find them until morning.

Hurry Lassie, hurry, Megan prayed silently as she lay still under the tree trunk.

Will's thoughts were identical to his sister's. But he was not laying still. He was pushing his full body weight against the mammoth tree, trying to push it off of Megan's leg.

"Just gotta work it," he said out loud to no one in particular as he wiped the sweat from under his brown bangs. "Just like getting the ketchup out of a new bottle."

Megan looked at her brother through new eyes. He no longer seemed like an annoying pest who always wanted to tag along and forgot to give her her messages. He seemed like a really great kid, who cared enough to work himself into a state of exhaustion to help her. Suddenly she felt really bad about teasing Will about his friendship with Lassie.

"Will . . ." she said slowly. "I never realized how much my teasing hurt your feelings."

"It's okay," Will grunted as he tried once again to move the tree trunk.

"No, it was mean," Megan said emphatically. "I'm sorry."

Will stopped pushing for just a second. He looked at Megan with a smile. "Thanks."

Honk! Honk! The noise of a car horn startled the McCulloch kids. Will stood tall and turned toward the road to see who was coming.

"It's Mom and Dad!" Will told Megan, who was lying too close to the ground to see the black 4×4 drive up along the side of the road.

Dee barely waited for the car to come to its screeching halt before she jumped out and ran to the fence. Dee headed straight for the gate, only to discover, as Lassie had found, that it had been locked shut. Dee grew silently angry. If only Arthur's men had locked this gate *before* the kids had wandered into the field, none of this would have happened.

Chris came up behind her and took her hand.

Dee looked out over the field. There, in the distance, she could barely make out the figure of a small boy.

"Mom! Dad! Over here." Will called out to her, shouting over the distance of the grass-covered field.

"Are you all right?" his mother called back.

"Yes, but Megan's trapped under a tree."

KABOOM! There was another explosion coming from far off in the field. It wasn't near the kids, but any explosion was not at all what Dee needed to hear. She began to panic.

"I'm coming in," she shouted frantically. Then she grabbed the aluminum fence and shook it with all her might. Chris put his hands between the octagonal links of metal and tried to lift it from the ground so he could crawl under it.

"Stay back! It's too dangerous!" Will shouted to his parents.

"Will . . . listen," Megan called to her brother in a voice so quiet he could barely understand her.

Tick. Tick. Tick. The ticking of the unexploded bomb was getting faster and louder by the second. There wasn't much time before it exploded! Megan was overcome with a sense of newfound love and a desperate need to protect her brother. It overshadowed all the fear in her heart.

"Will! Get out of here!" she cried to him. She

would stay alone. She could not let him risk his life for hers.

But Will's love for his sister was every bit as strong as hers for him. "No!" he answered her defiantly. Then, he looked around frantically for something to help him lift that blasted tree! Moving faster than he ever had before, Will broke a thick limb from the fallen tree. He jammed it under the trunk. Maybe the tree limb could act as a crowbar and lift the tree, he thought.

Tick. Tick. Tick. Tick. TICK. TICK. TICK-TICK-TICK! The noise was getting louder and faster!

Will could feel his adrenaline pumping with a power born of desperation and love for his sister. With what seemed like the strength of ten men he pushed down on the tree branch/crowbar. "Augh!" he grunted from his gut.

Finally, the tree moved—just a bit, but far enough to let Megan pull her foot free. Will grabbed his sister under her arms and pulled her to her feet. Without worrying about other shells, the kids started moving up the slope toward the fence.

From the distance, Chris saw the kids as they moved, Will helping Megan every step of the way. He could tell that Megan was in far too much pain to ever make it to the fence. He would have to get to his kids before there were any more explosions!

Without worrying about his own safety, Chris leaped into the 4×4, put the car into gear, drove toward the fence, and plowed straight through the gate, sending bits of aluminum chain link flying into the air.

Megan and Will waved frantically, trying to tell their father to stop. He was sure to hit a live shell and be blown to bits! But before the kids could get Chris's attention, a loud, almost deafening roar took over the sky! Chris stopped the car immediately. The kids froze in fear. What new terror could this roaring sound be announcing?

After a beat, Megan and Will summoned up enough courage to look up in the direction of the sound. There, in the distant sky, coming right for them, was an army helicopter. Will smiled with relief. Help was on its way!

The roaring grew stronger as the helicopter drew near, but the kids welcomed the once-scary noise. For a second, Will was sure he could hear Lassie's loving bark above the din. I must be imagining things, the boy thought to himself.

But as the helicopter went into a hovering position right above Will's head, the boy could see that he hadn't been imagining things at all. For there, sitting right in the open doorway of the helicopter, was his beautiful golden brown and white collie! Arthur Reynolds had had the good sense to drive to the nearby army base and arrange for an emergency helicopter to hurry to the field! Now a whole emergency crew and Lassie were here to save Will and Megan!

A crewman moved Lassie away from the doorway and carefully lowered a rope from the helicopter. Attached to the rope was a hammocklike sling, just big enough to hold two children.

When the rope reached him, Will helped Megan slip into the sling and climbed in beside her. The kids held onto each other tightly as the crewman yanked the rope up to the open doorway and pulled Megan and Will inside. The helicopter then flew upward and back to the army base, carrying Will and Megan to safety. Lassie licked their faces joyously the whole way back!

After he was sure his kids and Lassie were going to be all right, Chris backed the 4×4 onto the road, and opened the passenger door for Dee. Dee climbed in and the two held hands in relief as they watched the helicopter disappear into the horizon.

Neither parent spoke for a while. They were too busy counting their blessings. "Maybe it was a dud," Dee said finally.

"Maybe . . ." Chris began. But before he could finish his sentence there was an unbelievably powerful explosion in the center of the field—right where the kids had been! Flying rocks and earth filled the air. Trees blasted straight up in the air like giant brown and green rockets. Dee buried her head in Chris's shoulder. It had been a very close call after all!

Epilogue

Once the dust had settled from the explosion, and Chris felt that he could control his shaking hands, Chris and Dee sped off in their 4×4 without ever looking back. It would have been too much for either of them to have actually seen the deep, empty crater that the explosion had left behind. They did not need any extra reminders of the dangers their son and daughter had faced.

When they finally reached the landing pad, Chris and Dee hopped out of the 4×4 and waited impatiently for the helicopter to land. Finally they heard the now-familiar roar of helicopter blades off in the distance. The sound wasn't scary anymore, it was actually quite comforting. The sound of the chopper was an announcement that Megan and Will would be there very soon!

The helicopter pilot brought the chopper in

for a smooth landing. The crew members waited for the blades to stop their whirling. Then they opened the door and helped Will and Megan down and on to the pavement. Lassie leaped out of the helicopter herself and bounded joyfully behind, her injured hind leg already stronger and almost completely cured!

After a long, warm family hug, Dee looked carefully at her kids. The helicopter crew members had taken care of the first aid. The cut on Will's arm had been cleaned and covered. Megan's ankle had been wrapped in a cream-colored Ace bandage. Dee closed her eyes for a second and silently gave thanks that there was nothing seriously wrong with Will and Megan.

The dull purring of a 4×4 engine came up from behind the McCullochs. Chris turned around and glared angrily as Arthur Reynolds hopped out of his car.

"Thank goodness the chopper got there in time," Arthur said, smiling at Chris.

But Arthur wasn't getting off so easily. Chris grabbed him and looked at him with eyes full of venom.

"What is wrong with you, Arthur?" Chris belted out. "Those were my kids you almost got killed!"

Arthur did not move a muscle. He was already beaten by his own guilt. Nothing Chris could say or do to him could cause him any more pain.

"I'm sorry, Chris," he apologized. "I only had the area swept for shells once, even though I was supposed to do it twice. It was to save money."

Chris let go of him and moved away, as if he were repulsed by the man Arthur had become.

"What's happened to you, Arthur? When did you forget what was important?"

Arthur looked at his old friend Chris. Then he looked over by the black 4×4, where Dee, Meg, Will, and Lassie were standing huddled close together. His eyes grew watery.

"It all just fell apart, Chris," Arthur explained. "Ellen and I are getting a divorce. Kevin is a stranger. You're a lucky man, Chris. I only wish I had what you do."

Chris smiled weakly. He felt much kinder toward Arthur. "It's not too late, Arthur. You can undo what you've done."

Arthur stood up tall. "I'm going to. Starting now," he declared. "The job's still yours, Chris. On your own terms."

Chris's mind flashed back to the explosion in the mine field. He wasn't quite sure he ever wanted to see this place again. "I'll think about it," was all he could promise.

The two men shook hands, and Chris walked

back to the car where his family sat waiting for him.

"Are you okay?" Dee asked, squeezing Chris's hand for support. She knew it hurt to be disappointed in a friend's behavior.

"I tell you, after something like this, a man really gets to know his priorities," Chris responded, hugging Dee close.

"Hey, Mom," Megan called from the backseat. "I don't think I'm going to be able to do my chores for at least a week. Will's going to have to do them."

Will gave his sister a playful punch. "Hey! I just saved your life," he argued.

"So we'll get someone else," Megan giggled, looking right at Lassie.

Lassie barked at Megan and shook her head. She didn't mind walking through mine fields, climbing tall trees, jumping over high metal fences, or riding in helicopters to help Megan and Will. But doing the dishes—that was out of the question!